P9-CJS-501

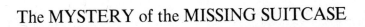

The MYSTERY of the MISSING SUITCASE

A Spotlight Club Mystery

Independence Public Library
Independence, Ore. 97351

The Mystery
of the
Missing Suitcase

Florence Parry Heide
and Sylvia Worth Van Clief
874-6581

Illustrations by Seymour Fleishman

ALBERT WHITMAN & Company, Chicago

With love to Chris Heide and his 1928 Chevy

Text © 1972 by Florence Parry Heide
and Sylvia Worth Van Clief
Illustrations © 1972 by Albert Whitman & Company
Published simultaneously in Canada by
George J. McLeod, Limited, Toronto
All rights reserved. Printed in U.S.A.

Library of Congress Cataloging in Publication Data

Heide, Florence Parry.
    The mystery of the missing suitcase.

    (Pilot books series)
    SUMMARY: When they pick up the wrong suitcase
through a mix-up on a bus, three children are con-
vinced it belongs to a criminal planning a bank robbery.
    "A Spotlight Club mystery."
    [1. Mystery stories]   I. Van Clief, Sylvia Worth,
joint author.   II. Fleishman, Seymour, illus.
III. Title.
PZ7.H36Myh   [Fic]   72-83683
ISBN 0-8075-5382-4

Contents

1 · The Hat Lady

THE FIRST PART of the mystery started on the bus. Dexter was half asleep. Long bus rides always made him sleepy. He opened his eyes as the bus rounded a steep curve.

He was looking into the eyes of a big green bird. It was a big green bird that was tickling his nose.

A big green bird? On a bus? On his nose?

Dexter blinked and sat up. He pushed the big green bird away. He pushed his glasses up on his nose. He stared.

The big green bird was on a hat. The hat was on the head of an old lady sitting next to Dexter. He had never seen her before. She must have taken the seat next to him while he was asleep.

The old lady was knitting.

Click, click, click went her knitting needles. And click, click, click went her teeth. She seemed to be knitting a long scarf. A very long scarf, thought Dexter. Endless.

The old lady looked up from her knitting.

"I'm glad you're awake," she said. "I moved next to you because a man on this bus is following me. He's after my money. If I sit next to you, he won't dare rob me."

Dexter rubbed his eyes. "Oh, I don't think anyone would rob you," he said.

"You don't believe me, young man. No one ever does," the lady said. She leaned closer and whispered, "I'll prove it. I'll prove it when we get to the next stop. Just watch. I'm going to fox him."

"Fox him?" asked Dexter. He wondered if he was dreaming.

"Oh, he's clever all right," the woman said, knitting away. "He keeps changing how he looks. His disguises. But he can't fool me."

She worked at her knitting. "See this scarf?" she asked. "It's all made of bits and pieces. Old sweaters. Old mittens. Old caps. I never waste anything."

She looked at Dexter. "Look at your sweater," she said. "It's wearing through at the elbows. That's just the kind of thing I like to use. If you are going to throw it away, do give it to me. I can make it into a scarf. I love scarves. They're very useful, you know. Everyone needs a scarf."

The bus was coming to a stop. "I'm just going to get out here for a few minutes," said the Hat Lady, as Dexter was beginning to think of her. She put her knitting into her large purse. "You watch me. He'll follow me. But he won't get my money. No-sirree-bob! Oh, he's a foxy one."

Dexter turned his head and looked back. One, two, three, four rows back. A man with glasses and a black moustache stared into Dexter's eyes.

Before Dexter looked away he saw the man's ears. They stuck out.

"Just watch," the Hat Lady said. "He won't get off this bus until I do. Then he will. And he won't get back on again until I do. Then he will.

You'll see. He'll follow me. Look sharp, now."

She walked to the front of the bus. She tapped the bus driver and said, "Don't go without me, young man. I'm going to have a spot of tea."

"Oh, no, ma'am," the bus driver said. "I won't leave without you. But we do have to leave on time. This bus will be here for fifteen minutes. Then we have to go."

The Hat Lady stepped off the bus. She started to walk toward the restaurant. The bird on her hat bobbed.

Dexter looked behind him. The man with the moustache stood up. Now he walked toward the front of the bus. He stared at Dexter as he passed. Dexter looked away, out of the window.

The Hat Lady was walking toward the restaurant. And the man with the moustache was following her.

Suddenly Dexter smiled to himself. If the man with the moustache was following her, then so was everyone else on the bus. Almost everyone was walking over to the restaurant.

Dexter shook his head. The Hat Lady was imagining things. But that didn't mean that he had to imagine things, too.

Dexter leaned his head against the window and thought about the last two weeks. He had had a wonderful time visiting Aunt Mary and Uncle Jim. But now he could hardly wait to get home to Kenoska.

His suitcase held arrowheads he had collected. Wait until Jay, his best friend, saw them! The boys had a pretty good collection already. But these new arrowheads were something special.

Dexter had sent Jay a letter about the arrowheads. He had written the letter in their new Spotlight Club code.

Too bad, Dexter thought, that Jay's answer in code had just come. Dexter hadn't had time to figure it all out. Now he wished he'd put the letter in his pocket and not in his suitcase. He could be working on it now while the bus was stopped.

Dexter reached into his pocket just in case he had put the letter in there. He hadn't. He took out a pencil and an old envelope and tried writing the names of the Spotlight Club members in code: Jay Temple, Cindy Temple, Dexter Tate.

The bus driver honked the horn. It was time for the bus to be on its way.

Dexter looked around and saw that almost all the riders had taken their seats. But not the Hat Lady. Dexter looked behind him. And not the man with the moustache.

The Hat Lady was over near the restaurant, talking to a little boy. And Dexter could see the man with the moustache standing near the bus, reading a folded newspaper. But Dexter could tell he was not really reading. He was watching the Hat Lady. The collar of his black raincoat was turned up.

The bus driver honked again. "Okay, folks!" he called.

The man with the moustache still waited.

The bus driver started the engine.

The man in the black raincoat still stood outside.

Suddenly the Hat Lady turned around. She walked quickly over to the bus and climbed the steps.

And only then did the man with the moustache put his paper in his pocket and get on the bus.

The Hat Lady walked toward Dexter. The bird on her hat bobbed. When she saw Dexter, she winked. "What did I tell you?" she whispered as she sat down.

Dexter watched the man walk toward them. He glanced at Dexter as he walked by. Dexter felt his heart thump. The man with the moustache really was following the Hat Lady.

Why? What for? Not for money. Not if she saved old bits and pieces of yarn. Dexter could not figure it out.

The Hat Lady took out her knitting and started to work on the scarf again.

"Where are you getting off, young man?" she asked.

"In Kenoska," Dexter told her. "I live there."

"That's nice," said the Hat Lady. "I get off

there, too. My brother is meeting me. He never believes me when I tell him someone is following me. I'm visiting him for a week. That's all I can stand. I never like being a guest. I have my own ways. And my brother doesn't always like what I do. Or say."

She kept knitting as she talked. The scarf seemed to be getting longer and longer as Dexter watched. He found himself only half listening to the Hat Lady. Before he knew it, he was asleep and dreaming of a long, long scarf. It was around his neck in his dream, and he kept tripping on it.

Suddenly Dexter jerked awake. The Hat Lady was poking him in the ribs.

"It's three o'clock," she said. "We're there. Look how much I did on my scarf while you were asleep."

Dexter rubbed his eyes. He looked at the scarf and then he looked out the window.

"Kenoska!" called the bus driver.

The Hat Lady opened her large purse to put her knitting away.

Dexter looked down at the knitting.

And he found himself staring at the most money he had ever seen in his life. The Hat Lady's purse was crammed full of ten- and twenty-dollar bills!

2 · All That Money!

DEXTER took off his glasses. He polished them nervously.

What was the Hat Lady doing with so much money? Was it hers?

And who was the man with the black moustache?

The Hat Lady must be right. The man was after her money. He must be. Well, he hadn't got it yet. And now, Dexter thought, the Hat Lady's brother would meet her. Everything would be all right.

The bus stopped. The Hat Lady snapped her knitting bag shut.

"Kenoska!" called the bus driver.

The Hat Lady leaned across Dexter to peer out the window. The bird on her hat tickled Dexter's nose and made him sneeze.

"There's my brother waiting for me," she cried. "I'll have to hurry. He doesn't like to wait in bus stations. Good-bye, young man."

The Hat Lady started to get up. Then she snapped her fingers. She leaned over and whispered in Dexter's ear, "He can't fool me! I have seen that man who's following me. He can't fool me with those disguises. I'll tell my brother. He'll nab him."

She started to walk toward the front of the bus. She held her hat so that it wouldn't slide off.

Dexter looked down at the seat beside him. There was the Hat Lady's big purse. The purse with the knitting, the purse with the money.

Dexter grabbed the purse. He looked up to find the Hat Lady. She was holding onto her hat. She had not missed her purse.

Holding the purse, Dexter slid out of his seat. He looked up.

The man with the moustache stood staring at the purse. And at Dexter.

Before Dexter knew what was going on, the man reached for the purse.

Dexter hugged the purse to him and jumped up. He pushed past people in the bus who were waiting to get off. He had to catch up with the Hat Lady.

The Hat Lady had just stepped off the bus. "You forgot your purse!" Dexter said in a rush. "Here!"

"Oh, dear—thank you very much!" she said. "That's why my brother worries about me. He says I'll lose my purse for sure someday. Well, don't you tell him. I won't. He'd just say 'I told you so!' "

Dexter saw the gray-haired man wave to the Hat Lady. She waved back. Dexter sighed. She'd be safe now with her brother.

But talk about forgetting things! Dexter

thought. He'd left that package Aunt Mary had given him for his mother on the shelf above his seat.

Dexter turned around to get back on the bus. Everyone was trying to get off, and he was trying to get on. He said "Excuse me" seven times in a row.

At last with the package in his hands, Dexter got off the bus. He looked around for the man with the moustache. He was nowhere to be seen.

Just then a voice shouted, "Hey, Dexter! Here we are." It was Jay.

Dexter turned around to see his best friend. And Cindy, Jay's sister, was there, too.

"Glad you're back," Jay said. "Things have been pretty dull around here."

"Dull, duller, dullest," Cindy said. "I'm glad your sister Anne let us come along to meet you."

Jay said, "The best thing in the whole two weeks was your letter, the code letter."

"You got your hair cut," said Cindy. She noticed things like that. It made her a good Spotlight Club member. She noticed a lot. That helps when you're trying to solve a mystery.

Thinking of mysteries, Dexter turned around to look again for the man with the moustache. Then he shrugged and turned back to Jay and Cindy.

"Wait till you see the arrowheads I have in my suitcase," he said.

"Did you figure out my code letter?" Jay asked. But before Dexter could answer, a horn honked.

It was Dexter's sister, Anne. She waved and he could see she was in a big hurry. "Hi, Dexter," she called. "Come on, let's go!"

"I'll grab your suitcase," Jay said. He started over to the pile of bags that the bus driver had set out on the curb.

"It's my old brown one," said Dexter. He and Cindy started over to the car.

"Hi, Anne," Dexter said. Anne was a pretty good sport even if she did complain. Maybe all seventeen-year-old sisters complained.

"The folks said that if I picked you up and if I pick them up, I can have the car later. Hurry up. I'll take you home first."

Dexter grinned at his sister. "Say you're glad I'm home," he said.

"I'm glad you're home," Anne said, smiling back. "But I won't be if you don't hurry."

Dexter got into the back seat and Cindy scrambled in after him. Dexter started to tell about the past two weeks.

"Where is Jay with that suitcase?" Anne fussed.

"I'll go and find him," said Dexter.

Just then Jay said, "Here I am. Sorry I was so long. Some guy was unloading boxes. Boxes and boxes. I think they were hats. And someone was taking pictures. Anne, if you give me the car keys I'll throw Dexter's suitcase in the trunk of the car."

"Not throw," Dexter said. "Place it gently. That suitcase has all those arrowheads."

Jay laughed and went to put the suitcase in the trunk.

Dexter looked out the car window. Suddenly he saw the man with the moustache again. He was waiting for a taxi.

Then Dexter stared. It was the man with the moustache. He could tell by his ears. But he had no moustache now. What was going on?

"Look!" Dexter exclaimed. "That man!"

Jay had locked the car trunk. Now he hopped into the back seat with Cindy and Dexter.

Anne was already backing up. Dexter pointed.

"Where?" asked Jay, leaning forward.

"Right there. The man with the black raincoat and black hat."

"Well, what about him?" asked Jay.

"He has no moustache," said Dexter.

"So what?" asked Jay. "Does he have to have a moustache?"

"He had one. On the bus. He had a moustache and he was following the Hat Lady. He was after her money. And does she ever have a lot of money!"

"Slow down!" said Cindy. "What are you talking about?"

"It's a mystery, a real mystery," Dexter said, staring at the man. A taxi had stopped and the man was putting his suitcase in it.

"You kids are always making up mysteries," said Anne.

"I'm not making it up," said Dexter. "That man had a moustache in the bus. Now he doesn't. It was a disguise. It was a disguise so that the Hat Lady wouldn't know him. She'd seen him some-where. He did have a moustache. I know he did."

"Maybe he shaves fast," said Anne. "People don't really wear disguises. That's just in books or on TV."

Dexter sat back. "Well, it's too late now. He's

out of sight." He spoke to Jay and Cindy. "It's really creepy. I know he's up to something."

"But now he's gone," said Cindy. "You'll never know the real story." She sighed. "I hate unsolved mysteries."

While they rode, Dexter told about the Hat Lady and her scarf and her money. And about the man with the moustache. Before he knew it, they were turning into the Tate driveway.

"Here we are," said Anne. "I'm going over to Beth's. Then I'll pick up Dad and Mom and drop them off at home. Don't forget to get your suitcase out of the trunk, Dex."

"I'll get it," Jay said, jumping out first.

"Thanks for meeting me, Anne," said Dexter.

"Oh, it's worth it," said Anne. "Now I get to use the car. Beth and I are going to a show tomorrow—a mystery."

"You'll go to a movie to see a mystery. But you never see one that's right in front of your nose," Dexter said.

Anne laughed. "The Mystery of the Black

Moustache," she said. "I'm glad it isn't under my nose."

Anne backed the car out of the driveway and the three friends started into Dexter's house. "Here, I can take the suitcase," Dexter said.

"Oh, as long as there's something in it for me, I'll carry it," Jay said, and started up the stairs to Dexter's room.

Dexter stood in the doorway. "My room looks a lot better than when I left," he said. "Good old Mom."

Jay put the suitcase on the bed.

"Wait till you see these arrowheads," Dexter said as he started over to the suitcase. He looked at it. "That's funny," he said, "it looks different somehow."

"Maybe it has a new scratch," said Cindy.

Dexter opened the suitcase. He stared.

He didn't recognize a thing. Where were the arrowheads? And what were these things in the suitcase?

It was the wrong suitcase!

3 • Who Is Mr. Moustache?

"This isn't my suitcase!" said Dexter. "None of this stuff is mine. What's going on?"

Jay looked at the suitcase. "Well," he said, "it looks like yours. It's brown. I bet the owner of this suitcase has yours now. What do you suppose he thinks of your arrowheads?"

"I guess we'll have to get this one back to the bus station," Dexter said. "I've got to find mine."

"Maybe we can find a name or address in this suitcase. Then we can call the owner," Jay said.

"He'll be glad to know where his suitcase is."

Cindy peered into the bag. She picked up a loosely wrapped package. Something fell out. Cindy screamed and started to run out of the room.

"It's a dead mouse!" she cried.

Jay picked up what had fallen. "Silly, it isn't a mouse. It's—well, it's a little wig. A man's wig, I guess."

Cindy came slowly back into the room. "I've never seen a wig for a man," she said.

"Well, now you have," said Jay.

"Say," said Dexter, pushing his glasses up on his nose. "Maybe it belongs to the man with the moustache. It must be his suitcase. Maybe that's one of his disguises."

He looked into the suitcase and whistled. "Look here," he said as he picked up a small plastic box.

Cindy and Jay moved closer and peered over his shoulder.

"A moustache," said Dexter. "A gray one."

"Look," said Jay. "All those plastic boxes have different moustaches in them. Five different ones."

28

"Wow!" said Dexter. "This really is a mystery for the Spotlighters!"

Cindy took one of the moustaches out of its box. "I always wanted to know how a moustache stays on," she said. "Now I see. There's a little place with special glue. You press it on and it sticks—like this! How do I look?"

"Silly!" laughed Jay.

Dexter looked into the suitcase again. It was divided into parts. One part had the moustaches and the wig. One part had a black notebook. One part had a camera. It was the notebook that Dexter picked up now.

"Do you think we should look in this?" Dexter asked. "It's not right to look at someone's private property."

"We have to," declared Jay. "We have to find out who the owner is. He'll want his suitcase back."

"And he can give me my suitcase," Dexter said. "I want my arrowheads."

"We have to find out why he wears disguises," added Cindy. "Maybe there's a clue in the notebook."

Dexter opened the black notebook. "Wow!" he said after a minute. "Listen to this. It's a list. A sort of checklist. It begins, 'Laundry.'"

"That's no mystery," Cindy said impatiently.

"Wait," said Dexter. " 'Laundry. Airline tickets. Timetables. Car.' " He paused and looked up at Jay and Cindy. Then he said, " 'Gun. Bomb.' "

"Gun?" gasped Cindy.

"Bomb?" asked Jay. "You're kidding! Let me look."

Dexter fixed his glasses and turned a page.

Jay and Cindy looked over his shoulder. Printed in pencil was a list of banks. And beside each one was a date: First National Bank, Orville, March 14. West Joney Bank, West Joney, June 1. Bloxville State Bank, Bloxville, June 25.

The three stared at the page.

"What does it mean?" asked Cindy.

Dexter shrugged. "I don't know." He looked up and pushed his glasses up on his nose.

"Names of banks. Names of towns, and then dates," said Cindy, looking again at the list.

"Orville. West Joney. Bloxville. Where's Bloxville?" asked Jay. "I never heard of it."

"I don't know. Somewhere around," said Dexter. "Not far, anyway."

"I wonder what it means," said Jay. He thought for a minute. "Maybe it's a list of appointments the man had. You know, maybe he's a salesman."

Dexter turned another page in the notebook.

It was a calendar. Some of the dates were circled. Dexter flipped the page back again to the list of banks. "Look," he said. "The same dates are circled, March 14, June 1, and June 25. And here's another. July 25."

"July 25?" asked Jay. "That's day after tomorrow."

"I wonder what it means," said Dexter. He adjusted his glasses and turned another page. There was a rough map drawn in pencil. He turned it this way and that.

"What is it?" asked Cindy.

"It looks like the map of a bank, I think," Jay said.

Just then the front door slammed. "Welcome home!" called Dexter's parents.

Dexter ran downstairs. "Hey, Mom and Dad, I'm glad to be back. Mom, you really did a job on my room. It hasn't looked that neat since I got back from my last summer vacation."

"Well, see how long you can keep it that way," said Mrs. Tate, smiling.

Jay and Cindy ran down the stairs, too.

Mrs. Tate was saying, "Tonight is this cook's night off. Dad and I picked up hamburgers and French fries and malts for everyone. Cindy and Jay, I've already checked with your mom and she says you can stay. We all knew you kids would have a lot of catching up to do after two weeks."

"Great, Mom," said Dexter.

"Say, thanks, Mrs. Tate," said Jay, and Cindy said, "That's wonderful."

"Maybe your dad can explain the map," said Jay.

"A map?" asked Mr. Tate.

"I'll get it," said Dexter.

He ran upstairs and brought the notebook down. "We think it's a map of a bank," he said. "We just want to know what all of it means."

"A new mystery, Dexter? And you've only been home a few minutes," laughed Mrs. Tate.

Dexter showed the map to his father, who said, "It does look like the map of a bank. See, here are two doors. And those must be the tellers' windows."

"What are tellers?" asked Cindy.

"Well, a teller in a bank is the person who takes the money or pays it out to the bank's customers," said Mr. Tate. He smiled at the three watching faces.

"Tellers," he went on, "are the men and women in the bank you see behind those special windows."

"Those windows with some sort of screen or bars?" asked Jay. "I remember that when I've been in the bank."

"Why windows with bars?" asked Cindy.

"Well, there's money in there with the tellers. The bank doesn't want anyone to reach in and help himself to it," Mr. Tate said. "That would be too easy."

He looked at the drawing again. "There are about ten places here for tellers. Then over here . . . well, this seems to show the special cameras. Security cameras. You can't really see them when you're in the bank. They are hidden. No one's supposed to know where they are."

"What are the cameras for?" asked Jay.

"They are set up so that they take pictures

when one of the tellers presses a hidden button. The button also rings an alarm, but not one you can hear in the bank."

"How does it work?" asked Cindy.

"Well, suppose someone wants to rob the bank. Maybe he gives one of the tellers a note. It says, 'Hand over the money. Don't yell or I'll shoot.' Something like that. So the teller hands over the money—but at the same time he pushes the button. The hidden camera starts taking pictures of the robber. Even if he gets away, there's a picture to help find him."

"You said something about an alarm," said Dexter.

"Yes, at the same time the cameras start taking pictures, an alarm rings in the office of the bank president. And sometimes at the police station, too. So unless the robber is very quick, the police come as he is leaving the bank."

"It sounds as if a robber doesn't have much chance," said Dexter.

"If everything worked right there wouldn't be

any robberies," said Mr. Tate. "But things happen, and robbers don't get caught. There have been several robberies right around here in some of the little towns. The robber got away every time, too."

"Do you know any of the towns?" Jay asked.

"Bloxville, I think," Mr. Tate said.

"In Bloxville?" echoed Dexter.

The three detectives looked at each other. Why had the name Bloxville and the date after it been written in the black notebook?

Why, unless the man with the moustache had robbed that bank?

4 · Three Banks Robbed

JUST THEN the telephone rang. Mrs. Tate answered it. "Oh, that would be fine. Let me ask him," she said.

"Dear," she said, turning to Mr. Tate, "the Andersons want us to walk over and see their new rosebushes and have a glass of punch with them in a little while. Do you want to?"

"Oh, sure," Mr. Tate said. "If I don't look at Hal's rosebushes, he won't come over to admire my geraniums."

He turned to Dexter.

"Don't you kids go working up any mysteries while we're gone." He winked at Dexter and his two friends.

"But, Dad, we do have a mystery. A real one," said Dexter. "I got the wrong suitcase and—"

"Oh, Dexter," said his mother, "the wrong suitcase! Call the bus station right this minute. Maybe yours has been turned in. Tell them you have this one. And as soon as Anne is back with the car, you take this one right down. Someone must be wondering right now where his suitcase is."

"I'm sure someone is," Jay whispered to Cindy.

"Well, I'll call the station," Dexter said to his mother. "But there is something very strange going on."

"You kids can have your hamburgers anywhere you like. Inside, outside, porchside, anyside," said Mrs. Tate.

"Upside," smiled Dexter. "We've got to figure out our mystery. We do have one. You'll see."

The three took their hamburgers, French fries, and malts and dashed upstairs.

"I'll call the station," said Dexter.

"I think we should sit down there and wait for him to come back for his suitcase," said Cindy.

"We could if the car were here—with Anne. But it's not, and she's not," said Jay.

Dexter phoned the bus station. The girl who answered said his suitcase was not there. It had not been turned in.

Dexter rubbed his glasses on his shirt.

"Dad said there was a bank robbery in Bloxville. If there was, and if there were robberies at—" Dexter flipped open the black notebook, "Orville and West Joney on these dates then it means only one thing. Our Mr. Moustache is a bank robber."

"A real mystery for our Spotlight Club!" said Cindy.

"Wait a minute," said Jay. "Remember Mr. Hooley's rule. We can't guess. We have to prove. What do we really know so far?"

"He has to be a robber," Cindy said. "Why would he have all those disguises if he wasn't doing something wrong?"

"Yes," added Dexter, "and why did he have a list with things like gun and bomb and airline ticket if he isn't up to something really bad? It sounds like a robbery and plans for a getaway."

Cindy tapped her fingers on the notebook. "I know," she said. "Let's find out if there were bank robberies at those towns. At those towns, on those dates."

"Well, how can we do that now?" asked Jay.

"At the library. It will be open another couple of hours," said Cindy. "We can look up old copies of the city newspaper. There'd be news about any bank robberies."

"The library!" groaned Jay. "I knew it, I knew it. Cindy always finds a reason to go over there."

"Well, how else can we find out?" asked Cindy.

"We can look through all the newspapers out in the garage," said Dexter. "Mom's saving them for some drive."

"The library will be quicker," said Cindy. "Anyway, everyone wraps garbage in papers once in a while and some pages might be missing."

Independence Public Library
Independence, Ore. 97351

"Okay," said Jay. "You win. Let's all go. It will save a lot of time."

Dexter looked in the suitcase again. He saw something in one of the compartments. It was a roll of film. He picked it up.

"Hey!" he said. "Look here. What do you think about getting this developed? If we take the film in now, we could have pictures tomorrow. They might help us. They might be a real clue."

"Someone else's pictures?" asked Cindy. "I don't know. It's like reading someone else's mail."

"Or looking in someone's notebook," said Dexter, holding the notebook up. "We can't stop now."

"Well, I guess you're right," Cindy said. "It's the only way to find out who he is. It's important if he is a robber to track him down."

"Right," said Dexter. "It's our duty." He put the roll of film in his pocket. "Let's go! We can drop this film off on our way to the library."

When they had finished their hamburgers, Dexter put the empty paper bags in the wastebasket.

"No one can say I don't take care of my room," he said proudly. "And here, let's put the notebook and everything else back in the suitcase and close it."

"You've turned into a neat kid," said Jay.

"A real housekeeper," said Cindy.

They ran downstairs.

"We're going to the library, Mom," called Dexter.

"The what?" called his mother from the yard.

"The library. To look up things about the mystery."

"The library!" said Mrs. Tate, coming into the house. "I wish your teachers could know. Going to the library, at night, during vacation!" She laughed. "We're just leaving to look at the Andersons' rosebushes. We'll be back before you are."

The three detectives jumped on their bikes. On the way to the library they dropped off the film to be developed. The man at the drugstore said they could pick it up at noon the next day.

After putting their bikes in the rack in front of the library they raced up the steps.

"Okay," said Dexter. "You're the expert, Cindy. I don't know where to begin to look for the old newspapers."

"Me neither," said Jay.

"You dopes," said Cindy. "You can always ask the librarian. It's usually Miss Beck. But I don't see her right now. Even without asking I know how to look. Come on, I'll show you."

Cindy showed the boys piles of old papers on shelves. "Let's see. The dates in the notebook were March 14, June 1, June 25. Right? The stories about the robberies—if there were any robberies—would be in the papers on the next day, like March 15 and June 2."

"Maybe," said Dexter. "It's worth a try."

First they found a newspaper dated June 26. They scanned the front page.

"Well, no news on the front page," said Cindy.

"It could still be in the paper somewhere," said Dexter. "After all, Bloxville is a little town, but a robbery there should be news."

They sat down at the table and spread the

newspaper out. Jay turned the pages one by one.

He shook his head. "No bank robberies."

Suddenly Cindy grabbed Jay. "Look!" she said. She pointed to a headline, "BLOXVILLE BANK ROBBED."

Three heads bent over the newspaper.

"At noon Monday the Bloxville State Bank was robbed of $5000. The robber, a middle-aged man wearing a gray raincoat and carrying an umbrella, walked up to Teller Eli Best's window. He gave the teller a note, printed in pencil. It read, 'Five thousand dollars. I am armed.' Teller Best handed over the money. The man walked out of the bank and disappeared before the alarm sounded. The police have given out a description of the man, said to be soft-spoken, medium height, about forty, wearing glasses. Police Chief John Neville blamed the bank's poor security system for the robber's escape."

"Copy it all down, Cindy," Jay said.

"Oh," said Cindy. "I've been promoted. Now I'm the secretary of the Spotlight Club." She began to write.

Dexter fixed his glasses. "This really proves it. It proves he robbed the bank."

"And probably the others, too," said Jay.

Then Dexter asked, "Are we sure? Remember Mr. Hooley's rule. Are we sure we've proved it? Just because he listed that bank and that date in his notebook?"

"Let's look in the other newspapers," said Jay. "Let's see if there were robberies in Orville and West Joney on those dates. That should prove it."

In an hour, the three had tracked down the other bank robberies listed in the notebook.

Every single bank had been robbed in daylight. And every time the robber had escaped. In spite of the warning systems in the banks. In spite of the cameras and the alarm systems, the robber had got away.

The three Spotlight Club members sat and stared at the papers and the notes that Cindy had made.

"I feel that we're getting close to something, but I don't know what it is," said Cindy.

Suddenly Dexter snapped his fingers. "July 25!" he said. "July 25!"

"What? What about it?" asked Jay.

"Remember—July 25 is circled on the calendar in the notebook. That must mean Mr. Moustache is planning another robbery," Dexter said, pushing his glasses up on his forehead.

Jay and Cindy stared at Dexter and then at each other.

"It's got to mean that," Jay agreed.

"And that's day after tomorrow!" said Cindy.

Jay said slowly, "Of course. He's robbed those three banks, and now he's ready for the next one."

"If only we knew what bank he is going to rob—we could warn the people at the bank," said Dexter, pushing his glasses back down on his nose again.

"So far, the banks have all been around here," said Cindy. "He must drive from one little town to another."

"But which little town will it be—day after tomorrow?" asked Jay.

"We've got to find out somehow," said Cindy.

Who was Mr. Moustache? And how could they find him in time? That was the problem for the Spotlight Club.

Cindy took notes on the other two robberies. Then she and the boys started out to the front desk. Miss Beck was there, sorting books.

"Hello, Miss Beck," said Cindy, smiling.

"Oh, hello, Cindy," said Miss Beck. "I didn't see you and Jay come in. And Dexter Tate! What a surprise!"

"Hello, Miss Beck," said the boys.

"What a funny coincidence," said Miss Beck.

"You mean that the boys came to the library?" asked Cindy.

Miss Beck smiled. "No, I mean that Dexter is here tonight. Did you get your suitcase back, Dexter?"

"My suitcase?" asked Dexter. His heart pounded. "How did you know about my suitcase?"

"Why, a man was in the library an hour or so ago. He was trying to find where you live. He wanted to give you your suitcase."

"In here? In the library?" asked Dexter. "But how—?"

"I know," laughed Miss Beck. "It does seem funny. But this is what happened. The man said he got his suitcase mixed up with another at the bus station. He was trying to find out whose suitcase he had. Coming here was the quickest way to find his own suitcase, he said."

"But how, why, did he come in here?" asked Cindy.

"Well, he was really clever to figure that out," said Miss Beck. "There was no name or address in your suitcase, Dexter. Just some arrowheads and other odds and ends. He said it was just like a boy's pockets, filled with everything under the sun. He was really very nice."

"But I still don't see why he came here," Dexter said.

"In the suitcase there was a letter someone had sent you. No envelope, so no address. But the letter was there. I guess it must have been from you, Jay."

"That was it," said Dexter. "Jay sent me a letter. It was in code. We were trying it out."

"Well, in the letter somewhere it said something about Cindy wanting you to know there was a special new book on arrowheads at the library. You could pick it up when you got home. Miss Beck would save it for you. Something like that."

The three Spotlight Club members stared at Miss Beck. Then Jay turned to Dexter.

"That letter was in code. The whole thing. Even the part about Cindy and the book on arrowheads."

Dexter took a deep breath. "He's broken our code then. That's how he could read the letter. And he came right here and—"

"Yes," said Miss Beck. "He came right here and asked me what boy I was saving the new book on arrowheads for. He explained why he needed to know. So I thought it was all right to tell him." Miss Beck smiled. "You'll probably find your own suitcase waiting for you at home, Dexter. I gave him your address."

"Let's go!" said Jay. "We've got to get there first."

Cindy turned to Miss Beck. "What did the man look like?" she asked.

"Oh, a nice enough looking man. And very polite. He was wearing a moustache. And glasses. He was carrying a black hat. I remember that because he set it down on the counter while we talked."

Dexter swallowed. "Did his ears stick out?" he asked.

Miss Beck thought for a moment. "Now that you mention it, I guess they did, a little," she said.

Dexter stared at Miss Beck. Then he looked at Jay and Cindy. The three quickly thanked Miss Beck and started out of the library.

"I hope we get there before he does," said Cindy.

"What will we do if he isn't there?" said Jay.

"What will we do if he is there?" said Cindy.

The man with the moustache would look in his suitcase right away. The Spotlighters were sure of that. He would know someone had taken the film. He would know someone had looked in his notebook.

He would know his secret was discovered.

They were in real trouble now. A bank robber might do anything. . . .

5 · A Warning

JAY, DEXTER, AND CINDY rushed out of the library and jumped on their bikes. They sped home.

Mr. and Mrs. Tate were in the living room.

"Oh, Dexter, you're too late. A nice man came to get his suitcase," said Mrs. Tate. "He left yours. It's up on your bed."

A nice man! The three friends looked at each other. That nice man was going to rob his fourth bank day after tomorrow!

They started to run up the stairs.

"One more thing," Mrs. Tate called. "When Travis Hackworthy brought the paper he said to tell you he wants you to take his paper route next week."

"I know," said Dexter over his shoulder. "I'm counting on it."

They raced up the stairs.

There was Dexter's suitcase. Dexter opened it.

There were the arrowheads. And some pants and odds and ends. And something else.

A big sheet of paper was there, covered with a strange message.

"What's this?" asked Dexter. "This wasn't in my suitcase before."

He picked up the big sheet of paper.

"It doesn't make sense," he said.

Jay looked over his shoulder. "It's in code," he said.

They all looked at it.

"Do you think it's in our code?" asked Dexter. "We know from Miss Beck that he figured it out. He had to read Jay's letter."

The Spotlight Club members stared at each other.

Dexter ran over to his desk and found a paper and pencil. "Let's hurry and decipher it," he said. "Mr. Moustache is trying to tell us something."

"Yes. He's trying to tell us something, and he wants to make sure we can read it and no one else can," said Jay.

"How does the code work?" asked Cindy. "If we're all members of the Spotlight Club then we should all know the code."

"We'll show you," Jay said. "We aren't trying to keep secrets."

"Keeping a secret from Cindy would be impossible anyway," said Dexter. "She's too good a detective."

"This is how it works," said Jay. "See, Dexter is writing down the alphabet."

"Look," went on Dexter. "You take the regular alphabet. When you want to read the code message, you just write down the letter that is two places behind the letter you see."

"I don't get it," said Cindy.

"Well, look. Let's take HYW. Look at the

alphabet. Take H. Two letters after that is J, right?"

"I see," said Cindy. "Now what about Y? There aren't two letters after that."

"You start all over at the first of the alphabet. Two letters after Y makes it A."

"Let me do it," said Cindy. "W. Two letters after W is Y. That makes J-A-Y—Jay!"

"But how could Mr. Moustache have figured out our code by himself?" asked Jay.

"Well, it isn't too hard to break an alphabet code if you have time," said Dexter. "You just have to know a few things. Every word has to have a vowel, so you know certain letters have to come up often. I don't know—I haven't really broken one. I've just read about it."

"Let's get busy on this message," said Jay. "It's got to be important."

They puzzled over the strange message.

"Z," said Dexter, fixing his glasses.

"That's B," said Jay. "And C means E."

"B, E," said Dexter. "W, A, R, E."

B-E-W-A-R-E! Beware! They shivered.

55

"I don't know about you guys, but I'm scared stiff," said Cindy.

They worked at the strange message.

In a few minutes they had the next sentence. "I, AM, ON, TO, YOU," read Dexter.

"I'm on to you," repeated Jay. "Beware, I am on to you."

"This is really scary," said Cindy. "What's next?"

Dexter kept working with the pencil. He talked out loud. "I, K, N."

"IKNOWYOURGAME," said Dexter.

"I know your game," repeated Jay. "Wow."

"Next line," said Dexter.

"YOU'LL NEVER FIND ME."

They stared at the paper.

"Beware. I am on to you. I know your game. You'll never find me."

"Anything else?" asked Jay.

"Seven more letters," said Dexter. "Here they are: D,O,N,T,T," he swallowed. "R,Y."

"Don't try," whispered Cindy.

"Wow," said Jay. "This is serious."

"Well. We're going to find him no matter what he says," said Dexter.

"But how?" asked Jay.

"And what will he do to us if we try?" said Cindy fearfully.

"Well, we're going to try anyway," said Dexter.

"How? How can we find out who he is?" asked Jay.

"Maybe the film will give us a clue," said Dexter.

Cindy said, "I'm so nervous I have to do something. I know. I'll get the paper and read Miss Tasha's column. Maybe that will help."

As Cindy ran downstairs to get the newspaper Jay said, "Honestly, if the house was burning down, Cindy would have to read Miss Tasha's column."

Dexter was thinking about something else. He said, "If only I could find the Hat Lady, maybe she could help. Just as she got off the bus she said she remembered who the man was."

"Forget about the Hat Lady," said Jay. "Let's figure out some way to track the man down."

"Yes," Dexter said. "Before he tracks me down."

"He has tracked you down," said Jay. "As far as this house to get his suitcase."

Cindy was back. She pointed to something in the newspaper. "Talk about fancy hats—I bet this one beats your Hat Lady's hat."

She handed the newspaper to Dexter. Dexter glanced at the picture. Then he grabbed the paper and looked at it harder. "That's her hat!" he said. "That's the Hat Lady's hat—and that's the Hat Lady!"

The story under the picture said, "Mr. Georges of New York, famous hat designer, arriving in Kenoska for a special showing of his hats, is seen here with some of the boxes containing his famous creations. Mr. Georges will be at the Bonton Store tomorrow morning with his new collection of hats."

"Why, look—a picture of my bus," went on Dexter. "That picture must have been taken just after we got off."

"When I picked up your suitcase I saw all those boxes," Jay said. "But I didn't think they looked very exciting. I guess the newspaper knew about Mr. Georges, though. Here's his picture the same day his hats got here. That's fast."

"Fastest newspaper in town," Dexter said.

"The only newspaper in town," added Cindy. "But that is pretty fast."

Jay looked at the picture. "The man who takes the picture usually gets the name of everyone in it," he said. "I bet they have the Hat Lady's name at the newspaper. We could go in tomorrow and ask."

Jay and Dexter looked at Cindy.

"You're elected, Cindy," Jay said. "All you have to do is ask for the person at the paper who wrote what it says under the picture. Then maybe we can find the Hat Lady's name."

"Yes, we have to find her because she knows who the man with the moustache really is," said Dexter. "If we find her, we find him."

"I hope," said Cindy.

"Anyway, let's sit down and write what we know," said Jay.

"I'm the secretary. I'll make the list," said Cindy. "I can tell better if I see it written down."

"Okay," said Jay. "You and your lists. Here's what we know already."

"There was a lady on the bus who had a lot of money in her purse," began Dexter. "She thought someone was following her. She said he kept changing his moustache. I didn't believe her, but she was right. He's the man with the moustache."

"Mr. Moustache," wrote Cindy. "Mr. Moustache was following the Hat Lady."

"Well," said Dexter, "and then he did take his

moustache off. I saw him without it at the station."

"And we found those moustaches in his suit-case," added Jay.

Cindy wrote: "He wears different moustaches to fool people."

"Okay, we know that," said Jay. "Then in his suitcase we found a notebook with a list of dates. And every date was a day when there was a bank robbery."

"Bank robbery dates and places in his note-book," wrote Cindy. "And floor plan of a bank."

"What else do we know?" asked Dexter.

"Well," said Jay. "We have his checklist. And on it he had written Airline ticket. Car. Gun. Bomb."

Cindy added the things from the list. "Now, remember Mr. Hooley's rule," she said. "We have to prove he wanted the gun because he robs banks."

"And the car," said Dexter. "To get away."

"And the airline ticket. To get farther away," said Jay.

"And the bomb," said Cindy soberly, looking up from her notes.

"Let's plan what we are going to do tomorrow," said Dexter.

"Okay," said Jay. "I'll pick up the film. It will be ready at noon."

"I'll go to the newspaper," said Cindy. "First thing in the morning."

"I've got to do some errands for my folks," said Dexter.

"If I were you, I'd be hiding," Cindy said. "Mr. Moustache knows who you are. He knows where you live. And he knows what you look like."

Dexter pushed his glasses up on his forehead. "I'll wear a moustache," he grinned. "That will fox him, as the Hat Lady would say."

Jay didn't laugh. He said, "Let's get started early tomorrow. We have lots to do."

"Yes," said Cindy. "There's no time to lose. He's warned Dexter not to try to find him." She shivered. "I think he's very dangerous."

"Well, we've got to find him," Dexter said, cleaning his glasses.

"No matter what," said Jay.

Cindy swallowed. "Okay, I'm trying to be brave." She looked at her notes. "He's going to rob a bank day after tomorrow. We have to find out what bank. We have to find him."

"Before he robs the bank," said Jay.

"Tomorrow the film. Tomorrow the Hat Lady. Tomorrow," said Dexter.

6 · Picture Puzzles

THE THREE DETECTIVES had a hard time sleeping that night. There was too much to think about.

Next morning Jay planned to ride to the drugstore and Cindy expected to go to the newspaper office. Dexter had errands to do.

By ten-thirty, Jay had finished his chores and was on his way downtown on his bike to pick up the pictures. Mr. Moustache must have missed the roll of film from his suitcase by now.

"They'll just be pictures of scenery," Jay told himself. "Just a lot of dumb old snapshots." But his heart beat faster as he walked into the drugstore.

"Here you are, son," said the man behind the counter. "That will be one-fifty."

Jay blinked. One-fifty? He didn't have enough money. Quickly he circled back home on his bike. He dashed upstairs and took the money from his bureau drawer. He hurried back to the drugstore.

After paying for the snapshots, Jay was so excited he couldn't wait. He decided to look at the pictures there in the drugstore. There was a counter. He could have a Coke and look through them.

Jay sat down at the counter and ordered a Coke. Then he opened the envelope that had the pictures. He held his breath.

The first one he looked at was too blurred to see much. Maybe it was a picture of a person. Jay couldn't tell.

What if all the pictures were blurred and fuzzy?

He looked at the next one. He blinked. It looked like the bank right down the street.

It couldn't be the bank, Jay told himself. But it did look like it. Maybe all banks looked the same. He'd never paid much attention before. He peered at the picture. There was a name on the bank, but he couldn't read it.

Jay quickly looked through the rest of the pictures. Two more were of the same bank—or was it the same bank? And was it the Kenoska bank? He'd have to ride over to the bank and take a look.

He was already starting to put the pictures in his pocket when he noticed one more.

It was a snapshot of an old car. It looked to Jay like a 1928 model. Maybe a 1928 Chevy. There was no one in the picture. Just the old car standing in a driveway, with part of a white house in the background.

Jay slipped the pictures into his pocket. He forgot his Coke. He forgot everything but the pictures of the bank.

He slid off the stool. He paid for his Coke and ran out and jumped on his bike. He rode over to the bank.

He propped his bike in the bicycle rack at the bakery. He crossed the street and took the pictures out of his pocket.

He looked at the pictures. Then he looked at the bank. He walked around to the other side of the bank and looked. And then he examined the pictures once more.

It was the same bank. Different views of the same bank, the Kenoska bank.

This was the bank Mr. Moustache was going to rob then! And tomorrow was the day!

Before putting the pictures back in his pocket, Jay glanced through them once again.

The old car. He stared at it for a minute. There couldn't be many 1928 Chervolets in this town. Maybe someone in that big garage over on Fourteenth Street would know whose it was. Or the other big garage on the other side of town.

Jay knew that Cindy and Dexter would be back at the house in an hour to meet him. In that hour he'd go to the garages. Maybe he could find out who Mr. Moustache was—before it was too late.

Because Mr. Moustache was going to rob the Kenoska bank tomorrow. Tomorrow. Unless the three members of the Spotlight Club could find him, and keep him from doing it.

While Jay was getting the pictures, Dexter had errands to do for his parents. The last one was at the post office. He had to buy stamps.

While he was waiting in line, Dexter looked around. There on one wall were pictures of wanted criminals.

As soon as Dexter had bought the stamps he walked over to look at the pictures. Maybe, just maybe, Mr. Moustache was already known to the police. His picture might even be posted.

Dexter looked carefully at each picture. Some were fuzzy. The clearest ones were those taken in jails. But the blurred ones were made from snapshots taken of people who had not yet been caught. There were no mug shots of them. There were only the old pictures to go by.

Dexter wrinkled his nose, trying to look at the pictures. He took his glasses off and polished them.

He put them on again. He looked at every single picture one more time.

Could this one be the mysterious Mr. Moustache?

Only the ears were the same. The face was much fatter than the one Dexter had seen in the bus. But maybe Mr. Moustache was thinner now than when the picture was taken. There were no glasses and no moustache. But Dexter knew that made no real difference. He puzzled over the blurred picture for some time. Then he read the copy below.

It said, "Richard Mann, 40, wanted for armed robbery. A loner. Scar on left wrist. Clever. Dangerous when trapped."

Dexter studied the picture. Except for the ears it really did not look like Mr. Moustache. But people change. And people wear disguises.

Dexter turned around, his mind on the mysterious stranger and the coming bank robbery.

As he looked up, he saw a man looking at him. Staring at him. Dexter fixed his glasses and stared back.

The man turned away quickly and started out of the post office.

A man in a black raincoat! A black hat! And ears that stuck out!

Dexter broke into a run. He didn't even have time to think what he would do if he caught the man.

Oops! Dexter bumped right into a lady with her arms full of packages. Packages scattered in all directions. And Dexter's glasses were dashed to the ground.

"See here!" sputtered the lady.

"Oh, I'm sorry," said Dexter. He grabbed his glasses. They were broken. He put them in his pocket and ran. He ran to the top of the post office steps.

The man was out of sight. Where had he gone? Dexter squinted without his glasses. Things looked blurry.

He ran down the steps. He looked up and down.

Then Dexter saw him. He saw Mr. Moustache. He was driving away in one of those old antique cars. Dexter could see that it was green.

Dexter ran for a block, but he couldn't catch up. And without his glasses, he couldn't read the license number.

He was out of breath. He felt for the broken glasses in his pocket. He'd have to leave them to be fixed. Lucky he had another pair at home, a spare pair.

Dexter got on his bike. Without his glasses, he thought he'd never get back home. Of all the times to break his glasses, just when there was so much to see!

7 · The Hat Lady's Clue

WHILE DEXTER AND JAY were having their adventures, Cindy was having one of her own.

She had ridden her bike down to the newspaper office. Now she walked in.

"May I please see one of the editors?" she asked at the desk.

"Which one?" a tall young man asked.

"Whoever would know about this picture in yesterday's paper," said Cindy, taking the folded newspaper clipping out of her pocket.

"That would be Miss Glass," said the young man at the desk. "Second floor, to the right, the second desk."

Cindy took the elevator up to the second floor. There were many desks and many people. Some of the people were walking around. Some were talking on telephones. Some were typing. Some were talking to each other.

Cindy looked for the desk of Miss Glass.

Miss Glass was a pretty young woman with long blond hair. She was going through some papers on her desk. When she looked up, Cindy handed the clipping to her.

"I want to ask about this picture," Cindy explained. "Can you tell me the name of the lady in the hat—the hat with the bird on it?"

Miss Glass looked at Cindy, and then she looked at the clipping.

"Sometimes we put the names in—if the photographer remembers to write them down. Sometimes even if he gives us the names, we don't use them. He took lots of pictures yesterday, human interest things. We used this one because we liked it."

Miss Glass looked at the clipping and smiled. "You're right. The lady's name isn't there. But that was a pretty hat." She spoke cheerfully.

"But I've got to find out who she is," Cindy insisted.

Miss Glass looked again at Cindy and again at the picture. "Don Needle took this shot," she said. "I remember when he came back he said something about hats. He said he had thought hats were going out of style until he saw all those boxes. And until he saw that lady—in that hat."

Miss Glass smiled again. "Don said that hat reminded him of something his grandmother used to have. A green parrot." She laughed.

"But you don't know who the Hat Lady is?" asked Cindy.

Miss Glass shook her head.

Cindy looked at the clipping one more time. She read over what it said once again. "Mr. Georges will be at the Bonton Store tomorrow morning with his new collection of hats."

Cindy read it to herself once more out loud. Then she turned to Miss Glass and said, "Thanks. Thanks very much," and started to hurry out.

"What for?" called Miss Glass, surprised. "I wasn't any help at all."

"Oh, yes you were," said Cindy gratefully.

Cindy ran down the stairs without waiting for the elevator. Surely the Hat Lady would be going downtown to the Bonton Store this morning. Surely she would want to see the hats Mr. Georges was showing.

Surely, surely, Cindy told herself. Anyway, it was worth a try.

Cindy hurried. In a few minutes she was parking her bike in the rack outside the Bonton Store.

Cindy ran though the door. She walked over to the elevators. There on a chart was a list of what was on each floor.

"Hats, hats, hats," Cindy said out loud. "They must be here somewhere." But she saw no word Hats.

She ran over to the clerk who was behind the glove counter.

"Excuse me," she said to her. "Where are hats? I can't find them on the list."

"Hats are in Millinery," said the clerk primly.

"Oh," said Cindy. "Thank you."

She ran back to the chart by the elevators. She found Millinery under M and read "Third floor."

Why doesn't it just say hats?" she asked under her breath. "It's silly. M as in Hats."

Cindy got in the elevator and went up to the third floor. As she stepped off, she saw a big sign:

Hats by Mr. Georges, East Wing

One Day Only, July 24

July 24! That reminded Cindy again of the date in the notebook. July 25. There wasn't much time. She had to find out who Mr. Moustache was before he robbed the bank.

Cindy walked to the east wing of the store. There were hats and hats and mirrors all over the place. And there was a lady sitting there, trying a hat on. Next to her was a long scarf. And knitting needles. It had to be the Hat Lady!

Cindy walked over.

A blond young man was standing behind the Hat Lady. That must be Mr. Georges, Cindy decided. He adjusted a hat on the lady's head.

"There, madame," he said. "That is the real you. Such style! So beautiful!"

The Hat Lady looked at herself in the mirror. Then she picked up a hand mirror and looked at the hat from the side.

"Oh, fiddle," she said. "That's not the real me at all."

The young man sighed. He lifted the orange hat from her head.

"Wait," he said. "I know just the hat for madame. I had someone just like you in mind when I planned it. One moment."

The man carried away the orange hat as if he were carrying a costly jewel, thought Cindy.

The Hat Lady put her own hat back on. It was the hat with the green bird.

Cindy walked up to the Hat Lady. She wondered how to introduce herself. She wondered what to say.

The Hat Lady looked up at Cindy. "They don't make hats the way they used to," she said. "Look at this one. I've had it for years. Never found one like it. And I've seen hundreds of hats."

"It's very pretty," said Cindy. "I like the green bird."

"Yes, it is nice, isn't it?" said the Hat Lady. "But it's getting a bit wobbly, I see." She glanced in the mirror. "I'll have to sew it on tighter."

The Hat Lady leaned near Cindy and whispered, "This Mr. Georges doesn't know a fig about hats. He's very famous. But he doesn't know a fig. Not a fig."

Cindy wondered how to go on. "My name is Cindy Temple," she said. "I was just wondering—do you remember on the bus yesterday—a boy was sitting next to you—"

At that moment Mr. Georges came back with a flourish. And another hat. "Now, madame, I have the perfect hat for you. Perfect."

He was carrying a gold turban covered with jewels. He took the hat with the green bird off the

Hat Lady's head. Then he placed the gold turban carefully on her head.

"There, madame! What did I tell you? Perfect. It brings out the sparkle in your eye. You wear hats very well indeed. If I may say so, you are made for hats, madame. Not many ladies these days can wear hats. But you, madame!"

The Hat Lady looked in the mirror. "It is very unbecoming," she said. "Ugly, for a hat. No, it is not for me. But thank you very much."

And she reached up and lifted the hat off her head.

"If madame just looks at it for a while—it is a different style from the one she has been wearing, of course. But so smart!"

The Hat Lady shook her head. "It isn't nearly as nice as the one I've been wearing." She sighed. "Maybe I'll never find one I like as much."

"Never say die!" said Mr. Georges. "I have a blue one that is you. You'll see." He darted off.

The Hat Lady turned to Cindy.

"About the bus," said Cindy.

"The bus? Oh, yes, I remember the young man," said the Hat Lady.

"Well, he said someone was following you," said Cindy.

"Oh, someone was. Very clever, too, with his disguises. But he didn't get my money."

"You knew him?" said Cindy. "Just before you got off the bus, you said you knew where you'd seen him before."

The Hat Lady nodded, and the bird on her hat nodded with her.

"Yes," she said.

"Where?" asked Cindy, her heart pounding. "Who was he?"

"Why, I've seen him in a bank. That's what I told my brother. He met me, you know," said the Hat Lady.

"But his name—or where he lives—or who he is?" said Cindy. "Don't you know?"

"Oh, fiddle, I don't know that. But I do remember seeing him in a bank. I've forgotten what bank. But he was there a lot. And of course he was the same man who was behind me in the ticket line at the bus station. He was spying on me even then, when I bought my bus ticket."

"But we must find him," said Cindy. "We must. It's terribly important."

The Hat Lady started to knit. Click, click, click went the knitting needles.

"Oh, it doesn't matter now if you find him or not," she said. "I don't have the money with me anymore. If he took my purse now, all he would get is my scarf. And my rubber bands and safety pins. I always carry useful things with me."

"But the robber—" said Cindy.

"Oh, fiddle. You're only a robber if you rob something. That man didn't get a thing from me. Just a long bus ride. Served him right. I was too smart for him."

Cindy didn't know what to say. This was the last clue. Now the Spotlight Club members would never find the mysterious stranger in time.

The Hat Lady kept on talking.

"I gave all that money in my purse to my

nephew. He wants to start a business. And he didn't have any money. But I had. So I brought him some."

The Hat Lady sighed, and kept knitting. The bird on her hat wobbled as she nodded and talked.

"My brother gets so worried when I carry money with me like that. Just because he's a banker he thinks all money has to be in the bank."

She smiled. Cindy smiled back.

"He doesn't know that for people who aren't bankers it's nice to see the money itself. Not just a piece of paper like a check. Anyway, my brother and I almost never agree about anything."

Cindy said, "But carrying so much money—that's dangerous. I can see why your brother wouldn't want you to carry so much."

"Oh, fiddle," said the Hat Lady again. "If someone wants to rob you, they'll rob you. A robber is a robber, whether for a pence or a pound."

Cindy thought about what the Hat Lady had said about her brother. "You say your brother is a banker?" she asked.

"Yes, a banker," said the Hat Lady. "President

of the bank here, or one of the banks here. His name is Andrew Pettibone. I'm his sister, Sara Pettibone."

"How do you do," said Cindy to the Hat Lady. "How do you do, Miss Pettibone."

The Hat Lady nodded. And the bird on her hat nodded with her.

"We have to find the man who was on the bus," Cindy said urgently. "The man with the moustache. He's going to rob a bank tomorrow."

The Hat Lady turned to look at Cindy in surprise. "By jinks and by hatters, you don't say so! Oh, I'll tell Andrew right away. Maybe he can help. He hates to have banks robbed. Doesn't like it one bit."

"Do tell him, Miss Pettibone, please," said Cindy.

"I will. Right away. Of course he won't believe me. Never does, you know."

"Oh," Cindy said. Then she asked, "You're sure you can't remember who the mysterious man could be?"

The Hat Lady shook her head. The bird shook

along with her. "I know I've seen him. In a bank. But I just can't remember which one."

Mr. Georges came with another hat.

"I'll have to be going, Miss Pettibone," said Cindy in a whisper as the young man said, "This hat has to be seen to be believed, madame!"

Miss Pettibone waved to Cindy as Mr. Georges removed the hat with the bird and placed a bright blue hat with feathers on her head.

"I'll tell my brother about the robber. And the robbery, whether he believes me or not," the Hat Lady called to Cindy.

She looked at the blue hat in the mirror and shook her head.

"I think it's a shame to have people robbing banks, don't you?" she asked Mr. Georges.

Cindy didn't hear the answer. She ran down the stairs and out of the store. She wanted to see Jay and Dexter. And find Mr. Moustache!

8 · Mystery Street Number

CINDY was riding into the driveway at home when Dexter caught up with her. Jay saw them coming and ran out on the porch.

"Hurry!" he called. "You won't believe what is in these pictures!"

"And you won't believe me," said Dexter. "I saw him! I saw him down at the post office! But he got away."

Cindy ran up the porch steps.

"I met the Hat Lady. Her name's Miss Pettibone. Her brother is a bank president," she said, then she looked at Dexter. "You look funny without your glasses," she said.

Dexter ran up the steps and the three of them went into the house. Jay spread the pictures out on the table.

"Look," he said. "They're all pictures of the Kenoska bank. The one downtown. The First National. I checked."

Cindy stared. "That's the bank where the Hat Lady's brother is president. We can call him and warn him."

"Or we could go down there and tell him," said Jay. "Look. These pictures prove Mr. Moustache is going to rob the bank."

"I have to go home and get my spare glasses," said Dexter. "I can't see a thing."

Dexter ran outside and next door to his house.

Cindy looked through the pictures. She studied each one carefully.

Dexter was back in a moment. "Let me have a look," he said. He looked at them closely.

"It is the Kenoska bank, sure enough," he said.

He picked up the picture of the old car and said with surprise, "And this is the car Mr. Moustache drove away in—just an hour ago!"

"Then that is his car," said Jay. "That should make it easier to find him."

Dexter squinted at the picture. "It's an antique. An old '28 Chevy. Green. In good condition. He really keeps it polished."

"There can't be too many green '28 Chevies in this town," Jay said. "If we find it, we find him."

"But let's warn the bank first," said Cindy. "Let's go down to see Mr. Pettibone and tell him. He can help us."

Jay put the pictures back in his pocket, and the three detectives dashed down the porch steps to their bikes.

In a few minutes they were downtown, standing in front of the bank.

"Let's just go in and ask to see the president of the bank," said Dexter.

"You ask," said Cindy. "I'm shy."

The three Spotlighters walked into the bank. Everyone seemed to be busy. Some people were standing in line at the tellers' windows. Some were seated at desks that were out in the open with just a railing around them.

Dexter finally went up to one of the desks. He waited a moment and then asked, "Could you please tell me where the president is? Mr. Pettibone?"

The man looked up. He smiled at Dexter and said, "His office is over there, son. I'm afraid he's not in today, but that's his secretary over there. Maybe she can help you."

Dexter thanked the man. The three detectives walked over to the secretary's desk.

She was a middle-aged, middle-sized lady with a friendly face.

"Your turn to talk, Jay," whispered Dexter.

Jay cleared his throat and said, "Excuse me, please, we wanted to see Mr. Pettibone."

The secretary looked up and smiled.

"He's not in today," she said. "He won't be in until late tomorrow morning. Can I help you?"

The three detectives looked at each other. Then they all began to talk at once.

Finally Dexter said, "We think someone is going to be robbing this bank. Tomorrow. We wanted to warn Mr. Pettibone and everyone."

The lady looked at the three eager faces.

"Well, well," she said. "What makes you think this bank is going to be robbed?"

"I got the wrong suitcase," Dexter started to say.

"You see," Cindy said, "there was a man with a moustache following Mr. Pettibone's sister. And then we found a diagram of this bank. The man had drawn it."

Jay stepped forward and took the snapshots out of his pocket. He put them down in front of the lady.

"Look. These are pictures of this bank," said Jay. "The man had taken them. We can prove he's going to rob the bank. He robbed the ones at West Joney and Bloxville. And now it's your turn. You've got to believe us."

The lady looked at the snapshots and nodded

and smiled. "Thank you very much," she said. "I'll be sure to tell Mr. Pettibone. I'll tell him the minute he comes in tomorrow. He'll be so glad to know ahead of time."

Cindy looked at the friendly smile. "Are you sure you believe us?" she asked. "Or are you just being polite?"

The lady smiled at Cindy. "Why don't you leave your names here with me?" she asked. "And your addresses and telephone numbers. Mr. Pettibone will want to write and thank you for telling us. And of course we'll take special care tomorrow not to be robbed."

The three Spotlight Club members wrote their names and addresses on the pad of paper that the secretary handed them.

"You'll be sure to tell him?" asked Dexter, fixing his glasses.

"I promise," she said.

They said good-bye and started out of the bank. "Don't forget your pictures," called the lady. Jay went back to her desk and picked them up. He put them in his pocket and thanked her again.

Cindy turned to look back as they left the building. The lady was looking at them and smiling. Cindy waved, and in a moment the three were out on the sidewalk.

"I don't think she believes us," said Cindy. "She thinks we're just some kids. We've got to find Mr. Moustache. We haven't much time."

"The old Chevy is the best way to find him," said Dexter. "Let's take another look at that picture, Jay."

They stood on the sidewalk and took turns looking at the picture of the 1928 Chevrolet. Cindy studied it closely.

"I don't know anything about antique cars," Cindy said. "But look here, the car's in the driveway, with a white house in the background. And you can just see part of the house number. It's on something like a little sign. Look."

She pointed and spelled it out because the numbers were written out in words. "Eighteen sixty-three Sev—."

"That's all it shows. Sev," said Dexter, looking over Cindy's shoulder. "The rest is hidden."

"Let's see, 1863 Sev," said Jay thoughtfully. "That must be Seventh Street. That would begin Sev—."

"Well, then, that's easy," said Dexter excitedly. "Let's go over to take a look."

"Wait a minute," said Cindy. "Sev—, that could be Seventh or Seventieth or Seventeenth."

"Or Seventy-first or Seventy-second or Seventy-third—" said Dexter.

Cindy sighed. "It's hopeless. Or is it?"

"Not hopeless," decided Jay. "It's a clue. We'll just have to write down all the possibilities. Then we'll check all the addresses."

"There isn't much time," Dexter said. "Let's not give up."

"We can find the house," Jay said. "There can only be a few houses in the whole city that it could be."

Cindy groaned. "On our bikes? Ride to all those addresses? Seventh Street is one thing, but

Seventy-seventh, that's all the way out at the other end of town. It's miles."

Cindy groaned again. Louder.

"But we've got to find him," said Dexter. "This is the fastest way. At least I can't think of anything faster or better. Can you?"

"No," sighed Cindy. "If only Anne could take us."

"She won't be back until tonight," Dexter said. "We'll have to do it on our bikes."

"All right. Let's write down all the possible addresses and then split up. We can each do some," said Jay.

"Split up?" asked Cindy. "Why can't we all go together? What if I found him by myself? What could I do, all alone? I'd faint. Or run away. Or something."

"Okay," said Jay. "We'll do it together. We can start with the closest address, Seventh Street."

"Good," said Cindy. "The Spotlight Club sticks together."

"Shines together," grinned Dexter.

"Or goes out together," said Cindy. Let's ride home and grab a sandwich. It's on our way out to Seventh Street anyway."

The three Spotlighters cycled back to the Temple house.

"Say," said Jay, when they were back at their house. "Suppose we find Mr. Moustache. What are we going to do then? We have to have a plan."

"Right," said Dexter. "We can't just find him. That won't do any good. Maybe we should call the police when we do. We've got to stop him."

"If we find him," said Cindy.

"Calling the police won't do any good," said Jay. "We can't prove anything yet." He thought for a moment. "But if we know who he is and where he lives, then it would be easy for the police to find him—after the robbery."

"Yes," said Dexter. "They could find him if they knew who to look for. But that would be after the robbery. Let's try to keep him from doing it."

"Let's say we find Mr. Moustache now," said

Cindy. "We watch him. We follow him to the bank. Then what?"

"That's right, we should have a plan," Jay agreed. "We could call the police. But by the time they'd come, it would be too late. He could make a fast getaway."

"We could hit him with something," said Dexter. "While we were waiting for the police I mean."

"He has a gun," said Cindy. "He might shoot you."

Jay broke in. "I know. Remember the TV show we saw before you left to visit your uncle? Where the bad guy was spilled?"

"Yeah, I remember," said Dexter, frowning.

"We tried to figure it out, but there were only the two of us. We didn't have anyone to practice with," said Jay.

"It all happened pretty fast," said Dexter.

"Like this," said Jay, jumping up. "Cindy, you be Mr. Moustache. Just stand there."

Before Cindy knew what was happening,

Dexter was kneeling behind her. Jay flew at her. He gave a big push. She fell back.

She got up angrily. "What was that about?" she asked.

"Practice. You were Mr. Moustache," said Dexter.

"I was not and I am not and I won't be," Cindy said loudly. "Practice on someone else. Not me."

The boys laughed. "Okay," promised Dexter. "Next time we practice you can push or be the kneeler-in-back-of."

"Good," said Cindy. "Then let's try it again. Now."

"The thing is," said Dexter, "if you practice being the one who pushes or the one who kneels, then you'll be the one to do it when the time comes."

Cindy looked at the boys. "No thanks," she said. "I'm not all that excited about doing that part. Or any part. If I have to be anything, I guess I'll be Mr. Moustache in the practice so I don't have to be anything when the time comes."

"I'd rather eat," said Jay. So the three had a quick sandwich. Then they got on their bikes to find the address. To find the house, and the car, and Mr. Moustache.

First they rode to the nearest address. That was 1863 Seventh Street. There was no white house. And no antique car.

"Okay," said Dexter. "Next stop is 1863 Seventeenth Street."

They started off. In a few minutes Jay said, "There's something wrong with my tire. I think I've got a flat."

"Let's stop at a garage and put some air in," said Dexter.

"Okay, but I think it's the tube," said Jay.

They put air in all three sets of tires when they got to the garage. But a few minutes later Jay's tire was flat again.

"Why don't I walk my bike back?" asked Jay. "You two go ahead."

"Not a chance," said Dexter. "Remember, we're all sticking together on this. We'll all walk our bikes to the next address."

They finally got there. But there was no white house. They looked at each other.

"We can't possibly make it out to Seventieth," said Dexter. "It's miles. Let's go home. Maybe Anne will drive us around when she gets back."

By the time the three detectives were home again it was dinner time. Anne was still gone.

"We've got to find him," said Dexter. "Tomorrow's the robbery."

"I know what we can do," said Jay, jumping up. "Let's call all the garages in town. We can ask if they have seen or worked on a green 1928 Chevy."

"Why didn't we think of that before?" asked Dexter, hitting his head with his hand. "We could have saved ourselves hours."

"And blisters," said Cindy, taking her shoe off.

"We'll call while we're waiting for Anne," said Dexter.

"The yellow pages in the phone book," said Jay. "We'll let our fingers do the walking, just the way the telephone ad says."

In an hour they had called twenty garages. Some were closed. But the ones they talked to said they had never heard of a green 1928 Chevy.

And time was running out.

9 · The Search

JAY AND DEXTER were still calling garages when they heard Anne come in.

"What a movie!" she said when she saw them. "Really scary. We nearly died. Beautiful!"

"Anne," Dexter said, "you've got to help us tomorrow morning."

"Whatever it is, I can't," said Anne. "I have a dentist's appointment. At eleven o'clock."

"We could start early. Please, it's terribly important. And I'd do the dishes for a week," urged Dexter.

"Well, that part is all right," said Anne. "What do you have in mind?"

"Just drive us around to some addresses tomorrow. Early. We don't have many left to check. But they are too far out to ride our bikes. We'd never get there."

"You're not still looking for your mysterious man with the moustache?" asked Anne, laughing.

"Please help us, Anne," said Cindy.

"All right. But I have to get to my dentist by eleven. If we can be done by then, okay. But don't forget the promise about the dishes."

The three members of the Spotlight Club called two more garages. There was still no one who had seen a 1928 Chevy. There was nothing more to do, until tomorrow.

Early next morning Dexter, Jay, and Cindy were ready to go. They all piled into the car and Anne backed out of the garage.

Jay looked at the list of addresses. "First stop, 1863 Seventieth Street," he announced.

Anne looked back. "Hey, that's way out on

the other end of town, chum. Just how many of these addresses do we have to check?"

"Not too many. And they're all pretty close together," said Jay. "Honest."

It was over an hour by the time they had gone to the first nine addresses. There was only one more to go, 1863 Seventy-ninth Street.

Anne looked at her watch. "Okay," she said. "This is the last one we'll have time for."

"It's the last one on the list," said Dexter, polishing his glasses. "It's got to be this one."

Anne drove the car down Seventy-ninth Street.

"It has to be here," said Cindy.

But it wasn't. There was nothing but an empty lot where 1863 should have stood. It was almost too much for the three Spotlighters.

"But it has to be one of those addresses!" said Dexter. "It has to be!"

Anne turned around and looked at him. "Maybe it's in another town," she said. "A town out in Kansas or something. And I'm not driving you to Kansas."

She turned the car toward town. "Well, we tried. And Dexter, you can't get out of doing the dishes."

Jay and Dexter and Cindy stared out of the window. "Sev—, Sev—, Sev—," whispered Cindy. "It's got to be in Kenoska. I feel it in my bones."

"Sev, Sev, Sev," muttered Jay. Suddenly he shouted. "Seville! Seville Road! Where we looked at those puppies one time."

"That's it! That must be it!" said Dexter.

"Now what?" asked Anne.

"Just one more try, Anne—1863 Seville Road," said Jay.

"What about my dentist?" said Anne. "I can't be late."

"This is it, honest," said Dexter.

"Okay, but you are right. This is it, the end," said Anne. "Now to find Seville Road."

They sat on the edge of the seat as Anne drove.

"It seems to be taking forever," groaned Dexter.

"You are so right," said Anne. "This is the longest day of my life."

She turned the corner and drove slowly along the street.

"This is the sixteen-hundred block," said Jay. "Keep going."

"It will be on the left side. Odd numbers are on the left," said Dexter.

"There!" shouted Jay.

And there indeed was an old antique car. A

green 1928 Chevy was standing in the driveway of a white house. They could hardly believe their eyes.

"That's it, that's it!" shouted Dexter.

Anne stopped the car. "Now what do you want to do?" she asked.

Before anyone could answer, the door of the white house opened and a man walked out on the porch.

"That's Mr. Moustache," whispered Dexter. "Without a moustache."

The man carried a large briefcase. Without looking around, he got into the car and started the engine.

"He's going to the bank," whispered Jay. "We've got to follow him."

"Follow him?" said Anne. "You must be kidding. If you think I'm going to trail some car all over the map—"

"But this is desperate, Anne," said Cindy. "He's on his way to rob the bank. Today. Today, July 25. We've got to stop him!"

"Look," said Jay. "He's heading the other way. Hurry up and turn around. We can't lose him now!"

"This is wild!" said Anne. But she put the car in gear, turned around, and started to follow the old Chevy as it moved down the street.

"Not too close," said Jay. "He might suspect something."

"Don't worry," said Anne. "All he'll see if he looks in his mirror are three silly kids and one middle-aged teen-ager. Middle-aged because I've aged a lot today just listening to you kids jabbering away. And driving a million miles. And thinking about the dentist."

"He's going to the bank. He's going to rob it," said Dexter.

Anne sighed. "You're crazy. You'll be the ones to get arrested. For disturbing the peace."

In a few minutes the old car turned into the parking lot of a garage. The man in the black raincoat parked the car. Then he walked into the garage. He had the briefcase with him.

The three Spotlight detectives and Anne watched and waited.

"It doesn't look like any bank robbery to me," said Anne, looking at her watch.

They waited. Suddenly the three detectives clutched each other.

Mr. Moustache was walking out of the garage. He reached into his pocket for something.

"Car keys!" whispered Jay. Dexter pushed his glasses up.

Mr. Moustache strode over to a black car. He was still carrying the briefcase.

He opened the car door. In a moment he was in the car and had started the engine. Then he backed the car out of its parking space.

"He's switched cars. He's switched so he can't be traced," said Cindy.

"Yes, and so he has the faster car for his get-away," added Dexter.

"Oh, honestly," said Anne. "He's just changed cars. That doesn't make him a bank robber."

"Hurry! We've got to follow him!" said Jay.

"This is my last chase," said Anne. "I'm going to be late as it is for my dentist."

"He is, he is, he is on the way to the bank," said Dexter as the black car turned and headed for town.

"Okay, and I am, I am, I am on my way to the dentist," said Anne.

"As long as you get us to the bank," said Dexter. "We'll handle it from there."

"But how?" asked Cindy.

"Let's see what his next move is," said Jay, peering out the window.

The black car did indeed seem to be heading for the bank. It turned at the side street and then stopped in the alley behind the bank.

The man in the black raincoat stayed in the car, behind the wheel.

The three detectives kept their eyes glued to him and to the car.

"Now what?" asked Jay. "Is he going in himself? Or is he waiting for a partner to run out with the money?"

Their hearts pounded.

Anne looked in the car mirror and shook her hair back. "Say, loves," she said, "I know you think he's going to rob the bank, but I don't. If he does, I'll do the dishes. But let me fly now."

Jay and Dexter and Cindy, their eyes still on the man in the car, filed out of the back seat.

"Bye, loves," said Anne. She drove away. The three Spotlighters stood back out of sight and waited.

"He's doing something," whispered Dexter.

"I think he's putting on a moustache," said Cindy.

"What should we do?" whispered Jay.

"Go in the bank and warn them?" suggested Dexter, pushing his glasses up.

"He has a gun," Cindy reminded them. "There might be trouble. I'm waiting right here, I know that. I don't want to be a dead hero. Dead heroine, I mean. Dead anything."

"There he goes!" said Dexter.

"He's put on a moustache. And another hat!" said Jay.

They stood watching as the man with the moustache got out of the car. He left the engine running.

"He's leaving the engine running for a fast get-away," said Dexter.

They watched as the man walked with his briefcase around to the front of the bank.

10 · "Stop, Thief!"

"Now what?" asked Jay.

"Let's turn off his car engine," said Dexter quickly. "Then we'll have him trapped."

He ran over to the car. He reached in and turned off the engine.

Then he ran back to the other two, out of breath.

"Here," he said, holding up the car keys. "Now he can't get away. We can get him."

"We?" asked Cindy weakly.

They stood against the building and waited. It seemed forever.

Suddenly everything seemed to happen.

The man with the moustache ran out of the bank toward the car. On his heels was Miss Pettibone, the Hat Lady.

She screamed, "Stop, thief!"

The man with the moustache froze in his tracks. He looked back at Miss Pettibone. Then he looked at the car. He stiffened as he saw that the engine was not running.

"We've got him," breathed Jay.

"But now what do we do with him?" whispered Cindy.

"Or what will he do with us?" said Jay. "Remember the gun."

Miss Pettibone ran toward the man. "There you are, you rascal," she said. "I know who you are now. I spent the whole morning in the bank sitting and knitting and waiting for you."

She looked over at the three detectives.

"Good!" she said. "Someone's here to help me catch you."

The man with the moustache backed up to

his car. He seemed to sigh a deep sigh. Then he reached up and pulled off his moustache. He leaned against the car and looked at Miss Pettibone. Then he turned and looked at the three detectives.

Miss Pettibone was saying, "I told my brother

you were a bank robber. He didn't believe me. Now he will. I'll go and tell him to call the police."

She turned to Dexter and Jay and Cindy. "Don't let him get away," she said. She ran back to the bank, her hat bobbing.

The two boys started forward. Cindy kept her eye on the man's right hand. What if he reached for his gun? What if he shot them all dead?

Mr. Moustache looked at the three faces. "Congratulations," he said. "I don't know who you are. But I do know that you're the best detectives I've ever run into."

Jay and Dexter moved closer, ready to grab him if he started to run.

"I don't know how you tracked me down," said Mr. Moustache. "But you did."

Jay whispered to Dexter, "Should we rush him?"

Before Dexter could answer, Miss Pettibone and a gray-haired man ran out of the bank. Dexter recognized him as the man who had met Miss Pettibone at the bus station.

"Good heavens!" said the gray-haired man. "What's going on?"

"You wouldn't believe me, Andrew," said Miss Pettibone. "But now you can see that this man was planning to rob your bank. This little girl told me about it."

She peered over at Cindy and then at Jay and Dexter. When she saw Dexter, she said, "You are the boy on the bus, aren't you?"

Dexter nodded.

Miss Pettibone pointed her umbrella at Mr. Moustache. "The jig is up, you bank robber," she said. "Andrew, call the police."

Mr. Pettibone turned to Mr. Moustache. Even if he had no moustache now, the Spotlight Club members would always think of him as Mr. Moustache.

Mr. Pettibone stood and stared at Mr. Moustache. And Mr. Moustache just stared: at Mr. Pettibone, at the Hat Lady, and at the three detectives.

Finally Mr. Pettibone said, "I don't know what's going on, but whatever it is, it's my fault."

"Your fault?" said Jay, starting forward. "But—but this man was just robbing your bank!"

Mr. Pettibone sighed. "I'm sorry for all the fuss, Sam," he said to Mr. Moustache.

Mr. Moustache smiled. "I hope these children —and I—and your charming sister—have proved what I told you. That's the important thing."

Dexter took off his glasses and stepped forward.

"Mr. Pettibone, we don't know everything about this. But we do know some things. We know that this man was following your sister. And we do know that she had an awful lot of money in her purse."

"And that's not all," said Cindy. "We do know that he had written down the times and places of different bank robberies around here. From his notebook we knew he must have been planning to rob this bank—today."

Mr. Pettibone looked over at the children. "He is not a robber. He is the head teller at the bank," he said.

The three detectives stared.

"He may be a teller, Mr. Pettibone. But he is

also a bank robber. He's robbed three other banks —at least three—and now he was going to rob yours," Jay said. He had to make Mr. Pettibone understand.

Miss Pettibone pointed her umbrella at Mr. Moustache and cried, "You snake in the grass!"

Mr. Pettibone coughed and looked down at his shoes. "Let's all come into my office and talk," he said.

"Talk?" screamed Miss Pettibone. "It seems to me there's been too much talk. Call the police."

"I'll explain," said Mr. Pettibone. He turned to Mr. Moustache. "I think we owe my sister and her friends the story about what is going on."

Mr. Moustache nodded. "We can't leave them with an unsolved mystery. Mysteries are fun, but unsolved mysteries are a terrible bother."

Dexter and Jay and Cindy stared. First at the man in the black raincoat and then at Mr. Pettibone. And then they followed the banker as he led the way to his office.

They all sat around a big table in Mr. Pettibone's conference room: Mr. Pettibone, Miss Pettibone who was the Hat Lady, Mr. Moustache, and the three Spotlight Club members, Jay, Dexter, and Cindy.

Mr. Pettibone cleared his throat. "First of all," he said, "I feel I owe you an explanation. And you too, my dear," he added, turning to his sister.

Miss Pettibone touched her hat and sniffed. "This man is a thief and a spy, Andrew. He wears disguises. He is pulling the wool over your eyes. But he can't fool me for one second. Or these children, either." She took out her knitting.

"We have proof, too," Dexter said, fixing his glasses. "We have a notebook that—"

Suddenly he remembered that they did not have the notebook. When Mr. Moustache took his suitcase back, the notebook was in it.

"But we have pictures," said Jay. "Pictures he took of this bank. And he was going to rob it. Today!"

"And he wears different moustaches," said Cindy. "So no one can recognize him."

"He's already robbed other banks," said Jay. "And the First National Bank was going to be next!"

The man—Mr. Moustache—looked at Mr. Pettibone and said, "Well, Andrew, who is going to explain what?"

"I'll start," said Mr. Pettibone. "You can fill in the parts I forget." He turned to his sister and said, "This is Mr. Scrimshaw, my dear. Sam Scrimshaw, the head teller of our bank."

Miss Pettibone looked at Mr. Scrimshaw sharply. "Maybe he is your head teller. But whoever he is, he's the man who was following me."

"Yes, I was following you," said Mr. Scrimshaw.

"See?" said Miss Pettibone. "I told you so!"

"I am a teller. That's true. I am not a robber. And that is true. What I am," and here Mr. Scrimshaw stopped, "what I am is a detective. A part-time detective."

"You're a detective?" Dexter asked.

"Detectives have a bit more fun than tellers," Mr. Scrimshaw said. "And robbers probably have no fun at all."

Mr. Pettibone smiled. "Mr. Scrimshaw was a private detective for years before he went into banking. He still does some detective work on the side. He likes to keep crimes from happening."

Cindy poked Jay.

Mr. Pettibone went on, "Sam Scrimshaw has been worried about the safety of the bank. He is on the Security Committee. He has thought anyone could easily rob us. He's been following the news of all the robberies nearby, in West Joney, Bloxville, and so on."

Dexter and Jay and Cindy looked at each other.

"He's been eager to improve our bank's security. But we have not paid much attention. We thought we were safe and that no one could rob us."

Mr. Scrimshaw shook his head. "It's so easy to feel safe if nothing happens. But an ounce of prevention is worth a pound of crime."

"Sam has been trying to change our thinking about safety. And he has—"

"But he was the one who was trying to get my money on the bus, Andrew," said Miss Pettibone, knitting away. "I never forget a face. With or without a moustache."

"But he was following you because I asked him to," said Mr. Pettibone.

"Asked him to?" said Dexter.

"Asked him to?" said Miss Pettibone.

"I don't understand," said Dexter.

Mr. Pettibone gave a little smile and said, "Well, my sister was carrying a lot of money, as you know. She wanted to give it to our nephew to start his own business. I didn't approve. But she wanted to do it. And she does get her own way, of course. But I was worried. So was Sam. He offered to keep an eye on her. He thought she might recognize him from the bank so he kept changing his moustache."

"Well, I never!" said Miss Pettibone. "Really, Andrew—having me followed and not telling me!"

"I still don't understand it all," said Jay.

"He tried to scare us," said Dexter, pushing his glasses up on his forehead. "He warned us in code to beware."

Mr. Scrimshaw took a deep breath. "Well,

123

when I figured out your code, I thought it would be fun to make a mystery for you. Sometime later, I was going to send another code letter to explain. I never guessed that you and your friends would track me down—and in a very clever way indeed."

He turned to the three detectives and asked them, "How did you find me? How did you figure things out?"

Jay explained about the film, about the picture of the old car, and about the address.

"We finally found the right house. You were just leaving so we followed you," said Cindy.

Mr. Scrimshaw nodded. "Clever, very clever."

"What about changing cars?" asked Jay.

"I changed cars because I was leaving my old Chevy for some work."

"You left the engine in the other car running," said Jay, and Cindy added, "To make a quick get-away, we thought."

"No. The battery has been giving me a lot of trouble and that's why I left the car running. Maybe I'll never get it started again now. But it doesn't matter. This is much more important."

"Your list!" said Dexter. "The gun, the bomb."

Mr. Scrimshaw frowned. "The gun is for target practice. It's a hobby. The bomb?" He raised his eyebrows. "Oh, I know, an insect bomb. I always take one on trips, and I'm going on a trip. I've made my reservations and everything."

Mr. Pettibone cleared his throat. "It seems to me that we have some very sharp detectives here."

"Yes," said Mr. Scrimshaw. He turned to the Spotlight Club members. "You've been very helpful. In the first place, if it hadn't been for you—and if I had been a robber—I would have got away with it."

"As I now see," said Mr. Pettibone.

Mr. Scrimshaw smiled and reached in his pocket. He took out a moustache and held it up.

He went on, "I went into the bank, where I've worked for years, a few minutes ago. I wore this moustache. And not one single person recognized me. Except Miss Pettibone. If I had been a robber, I could have escaped—except for Miss Pettibone and you three detectives."

"It's my idea," said Mr. Pettibone, "after seeing how these young people acted, that perhaps they would help you on the Security Committee."

"I was just thinking of that," said Mr. Scrimshaw.

He spoke to everyone. "The fact that I am not the robber does not mean there is no robber. A robber might be planning to rob this bank this very week. This very day. I would be happy to meet with you right away to see what can be done to stop such a thing."

"What about a luncheon meeting with the three new members of the bank Security Committee?" asked Mr. Pettibone.

Cindy swallowed. "Can Miss Pettibone come, too?" she asked. "To the luncheon meeting, I mean?"

"Of course," said Mr. Scrimshaw, "if she has forgiven me for following her."

Miss Pettibone looked up from her knitting. "It added a bit of excitement to the trip," she admitted. Then she looked down at her scarf. "There! The scarf is finished! Here, young lady," she said to Cindy, "you may have it. It's all yours."

"Oh, thank you," said Cindy. She put the scarf around her neck.

"The mystery of the missing suitcase, solved!" said Jay.

"Wait till Anne hears about this," said Dexter.

"Have you ever heard of a Security Committee doing dishes?" laughed Jay.

Independence Public Library
Independence, Ore. 97351

About the Authors and Artist

Will Florence Parry Heide and Sylvia Worth Van, Clief become the Ellery Queen of juvenile mysteries? One thing is sure, they're thoroughly enjoying the challenge of collaborating on the puzzles that make the Spotlight Club stories good reading. And they confess they, too, are sometimes mystified until the plot twists take the right turn.

Mrs. Heide and Mrs. Van Clief, both of Kenosha, Wisconsin, began to write together when Mrs. Heide supplied the lyrics for children's songs written by Mrs. Van Clief. They worked together on a musical for girls and boys and another for television before turning to picture books. Mrs. Heide is also known for a wide range of juvenile fiction which includes *The Shrinking of Treehorn, The Color of Rain,* and *The Key.*

In the first of the Spotlight Club stories, the authors introduced Dexter, Jay, and Cindy and Mr. Hooley's famous (or to-become-famous) rule—you have to prove something, not just guess. And they incidentally proved how to write an easy, fun-to-read mystery.

◆◆◆

Seymour Fleishman won't say who was his model for the Hat Lady in *The Mystery of the Missing Suitcase* nor where she got her marvelous parrot hat. In his studio in his Chicago home, Mr. Fleishman illustrates picture books, textbooks, magazine features, and sometimes new editions of classics such as the *Peterkin Papers.* He has been author as well as artist and written three picture books. Once he undertook publishing and founded the March Hare Press, whose author was the pseudonymous Mr. Fough. That's a name that defies pronunciation, although it just may rhyme with "through."